S0-BWQ-716

STATE PROFILES

LOUISIANA

BY NATHAN SOMMER

BLASTOFF!
DISCOVERY

BELLWETHER MEDIA • MINNEAPOLIS, MN

Blastoff! Discovery launches a new mission: reading to learn. Filled with facts and features, each book offers you an exciting new world to explore!

BLASTOFF! UNIVERSE

BLASTOFF! Beginners — GRADE K

BLASTOFF! READERS — GRADES 1-3

BLASTOFF! DISCOVERY — GRADE 4

This edition first published in 2022 by Bellwether Media, Inc.

No part of this publication may be reproduced in whole or in part without written permission of the publisher.
For information regarding permission, write to Bellwether Media, Inc., Attention: Permissions Department,
6012 Blue Circle Drive, Minnetonka, MN 55343.

Library of Congress Cataloging-in-Publication Data

Names: Sommer, Nathan, author.
Title: Louisiana / Nathan Sommer.
Description: Minneapolis, MN : Bellwether Media, 2022. |
 Series: Blastoff! Discovery: State profiles | Includes bibliographical
 references and index. | Audience: Ages 7-13 | Audience: Grades
 4-6 | Summary: "Engaging images accompany information
 about Louisiana. The combination of high-interest subject matter and
 narrative text is intended for students in grades 3 through 8"
 Provided by publisher.
Identifiers: LCCN 2021019658 (print) | LCCN 2021019659 (ebook)
 | ISBN 9781644873892 (library binding) |
 ISBN 9781648341663 (ebook)
Subjects: LCSH: Louisiana–Juvenile literature.
Classification: LCC F369.3 .S66 2022 (print) | LCC F369.3 (ebook)
 | DDC 976.3–dc23
LC record available at https://lccn.loc.gov/2021019658
LC ebook record available at https://lccn.loc.gov/2021019659

Editor: Colleen Sexton   Designer: Laura Sowers

Printed in the United States of America, North Mankato, MN.

TABLE OF CONTENTS

A family begins a day out in New Orleans. Right away, they notice the energy on Canal Street. Music and people keep this street buzzing! The family hops on a streetcar. It heads down mansion-filled Saint Charles Avenue. Some homes there date back to the 1800s!

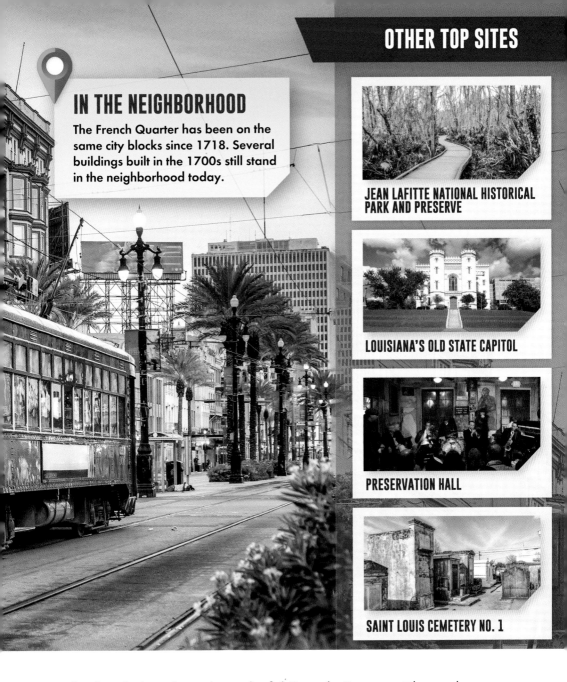

IN THE NEIGHBORHOOD

The French Quarter has been on the same city blocks since 1718. Several buildings built in the 1700s still stand in the neighborhood today.

JEAN LAFITTE NATIONAL HISTORICAL PARK AND PRESERVE

LOUISIANA'S OLD STATE CAPITOL

PRESERVATION HALL

SAINT LOUIS CEMETERY NO. 1

The family heads to the colorful French Quarter. There, they stop at historic Jackson Square. They enjoy soulful jazz music in the shadow of the Saint Louis **Cathedral**. In Woldenberg Park, the family watches ships cruise down the Mississippi River. They cap off their day with sweet *beignets* at Café Du Monde. Welcome to Louisiana!

Louisiana lies in the southern United States. The Sabine River flows along part of the state's western border with Texas. Arkansas is Louisiana's neighbor to the north. The Mississippi River forms much of Louisiana's eastern border with Mississippi. The river empties into the **Gulf** of Mexico, which washes the state's southern shore. Islands dot the waters off the coast.

Louisiana is shaped like a boot. It covers 52,378 square miles (135,659 square kilometers). The capital, Baton Rouge, sits on the Mississippi River in southeastern Louisiana. Other major cities include New Orleans, Lafayette, and Lake Charles in the south and Shreveport in the north.

SHREVEPORT

SABINE RIVER

TEXAS

LAKE CHARLES

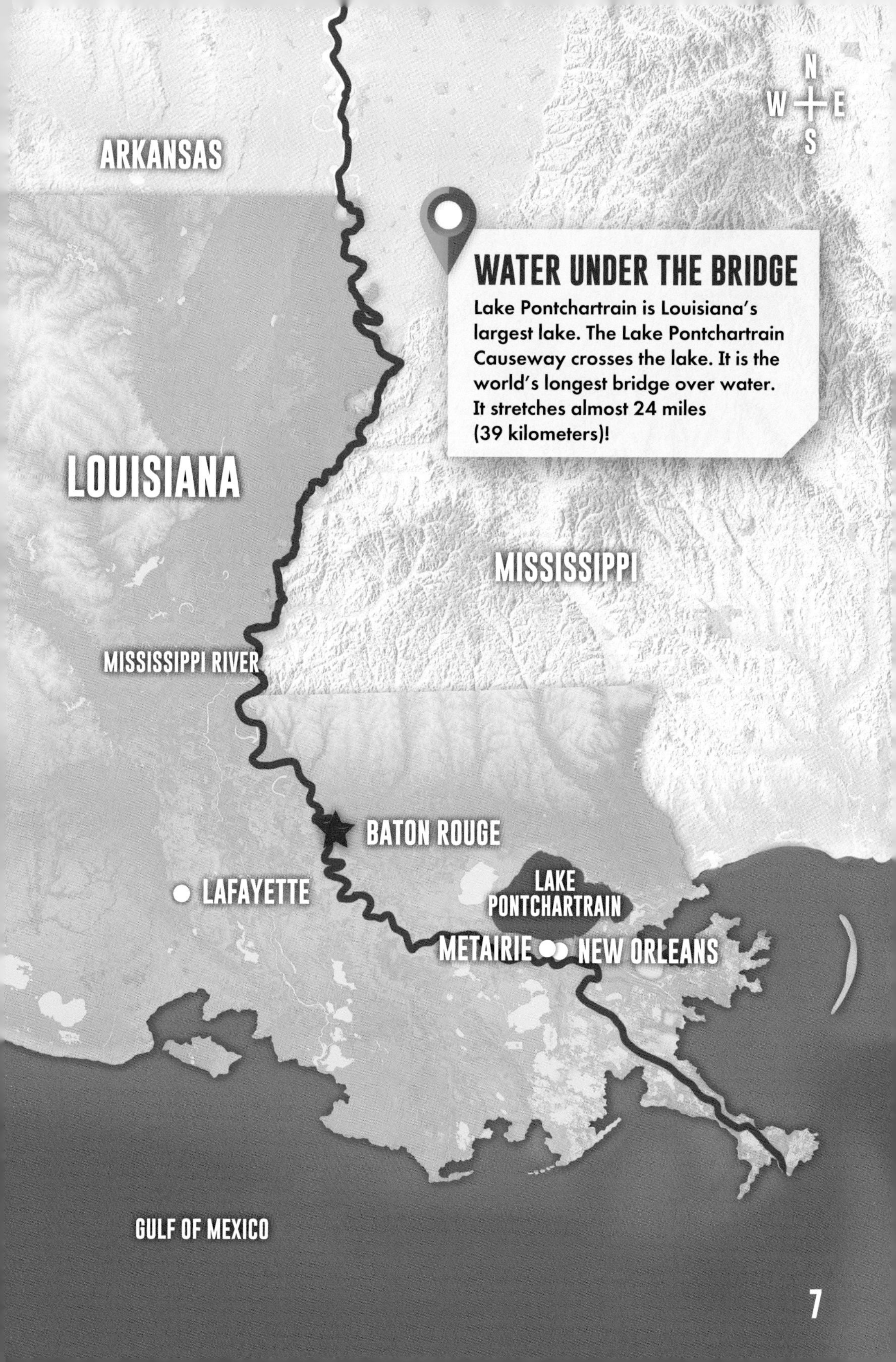

ARKANSAS

N
W + E
S

WATER UNDER THE BRIDGE

Lake Pontchartrain is Louisiana's largest lake. The Lake Pontchartrain Causeway crosses the lake. It is the world's longest bridge over water. It stretches almost 24 miles (39 kilometers)!

LOUISIANA

MISSISSIPPI

MISSISSIPPI RIVER

BATON ROUGE

LAFAYETTE

LAKE PONTCHARTRAIN

METAIRIE ●● NEW ORLEANS

GULF OF MEXICO

People arrived in Louisiana more than 10,000 years ago. In time, they built villages that featured earthen mounds. Many villagers died of diseases brought by European explorers. The survivors formed tribes that included the Choctaw, Chitimacha, and Tunica peoples.

THE ACADIANS

In the 1750s, British soldiers drove French settlers called Acadians out of Canada. Many Acadians settled in what is now Louisiana. Today, the state's Cajun residents trace their roots to the Acadians.

Spain first explored Louisiana in 1541. The French claimed it in 1682. France's Natchitoches became the first permanent **settlement**. Soon, more settlements popped up along the Mississippi River. Farmers built **plantations**. They used **enslaved** Africans to produce cotton and sugarcane. The United States bought Louisiana in 1803 as a part of the **Louisiana Purchase**. It became the 18th state in 1812.

NATIVE PEOPLES OF LOUISIANA

COUSHATTA TRIBE OF LOUISIANA

- Original lands in Tennessee, Georgia, and Alabama
- Moved farther south and west to avoid European settlers
- About 865 in Louisiana today

JENA BAND OF CHOCTAW INDIANS

- Original lands in Mississippi
- Settled in Louisiana in the 1800s
- More than 320 in Louisiana today

CHITIMACHA TRIBE OF LOUISIANA

- Original lands in southeastern Louisiana
- The only tribe in Louisiana to still live on part of their original lands
- About 1,300 in Louisiana today

TUNICA-BILOXI TRIBE OF LOUISIANA

- Biloxi people from Mississippi and Alabama joined the Tunica tribe in Louisiana in the early 1800s
- More than 500 Tunica-Biloxi in Louisiana today

Much of Louisiana is coastal **plains**. These regions are flat with many lakes and rivers. The Mississippi River formed the Mississippi **Delta** region. The river carried sand and rocks that built up over time. Now, this area of swamps and **bayous** covers southern Louisiana. It drains into the Gulf of Mexico.

MISSISSIPPI RIVER

■ MISSISSIPPI DELTA
□ ATCHAFALAYA BASIN

The Delta is also home to the Atchafalaya **Basin**, the country's largest swamp. The land rises to the north into rolling hills and grassy **prairies**.

MISSISSIPPI RIVER DELTA

LOUISIANA'S CHALLENGE: CLIMATE CHANGE

Climate change affects Louisiana in many ways. Warming seas make powerful hurricanes more likely. Rising sea levels wear away the state's beaches and flood its bayous. Louisiana loses about a football field of land each hour.

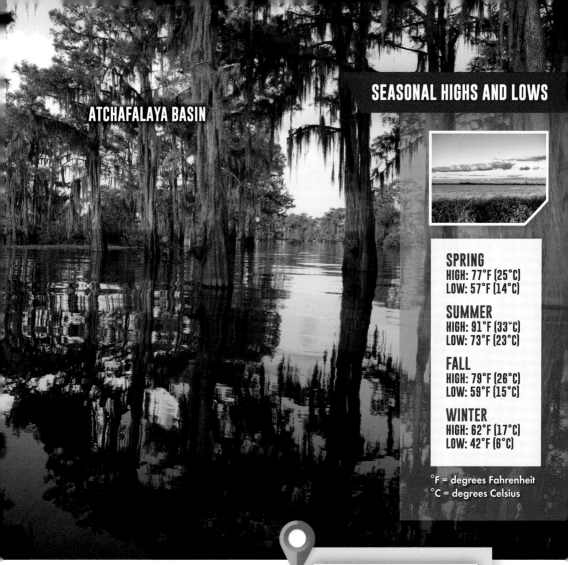

ATCHAFALAYA BASIN

SEASONAL HIGHS AND LOWS

SPRING
HIGH: 77°F (25°C)
LOW: 57°F (14°C)

SUMMER
HIGH: 91°F (33°C)
LOW: 73°F (23°C)

FALL
HIGH: 79°F (26°C)
LOW: 59°F (15°C)

WINTER
HIGH: 62°F (17°C)
LOW: 42°F (6°C)

°F = degrees Fahrenheit
°C = degrees Celsius

Louisiana's summers are hot, muggy, and rainy. Winters are mild. Louisianans must be prepared for **hurricanes** during the warmer seasons.

HURRICANE KATRINA

One of the deadliest hurricanes in U.S. history struck Louisiana in 2005. Hurricane Katrina took more than 1,000 lives and left hundreds of thousands of people homeless.

Alligators reign in Louisiana's bayous. These large reptiles hunt down muskrats, wild hogs, and gray foxes. Catfish, bass, and sunfish swim in bayou waters. Cottonmouth snakes glide through the water to catch fish and birds. Ospreys and great blue herons feast on fish, crabs, and frogs.

Coastal marshes draw ducks and geese in winter. Louisiana's state bird, the brown pelican, scoops up fish along the shore. Bull sharks, stingrays, and manatees swim in Louisiana's coastal waters. Northern Louisiana's prairies and woodlands shelter deer, opossums, and skunks. In forests, Louisiana black bears search for nuts and berries.

MANATEE

OSPREY

WILD HOG

BULL SHARK

BROWN PELICAN

AMERICAN ALLIGATOR

Life Span: up to 50 years
Status: least concern

American alligator range =

LEAST CONCERN	NEAR THREATENED	VULNERABLE	ENDANGERED	CRITICALLY ENDANGERED	EXTINCT IN THE WILD	EXTINCT

13

More than 4.6 million Louisianans call the state home. About four out of five live in cities. Most city dwellers live in and around New Orleans. Many residents of central and northern Louisiana live in **rural** areas.

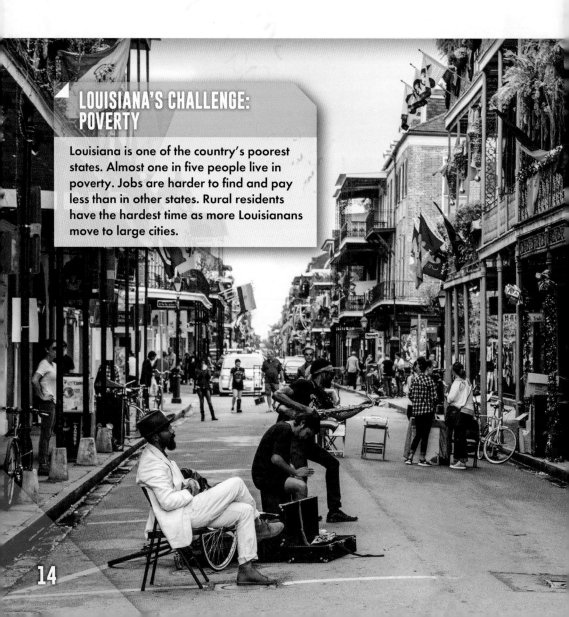

LOUISIANA'S CHALLENGE: POVERTY

Louisiana is one of the country's poorest states. Almost one in five people live in poverty. Jobs are harder to find and pay less than in other states. Rural residents have the hardest time as more Louisianans move to large cities.

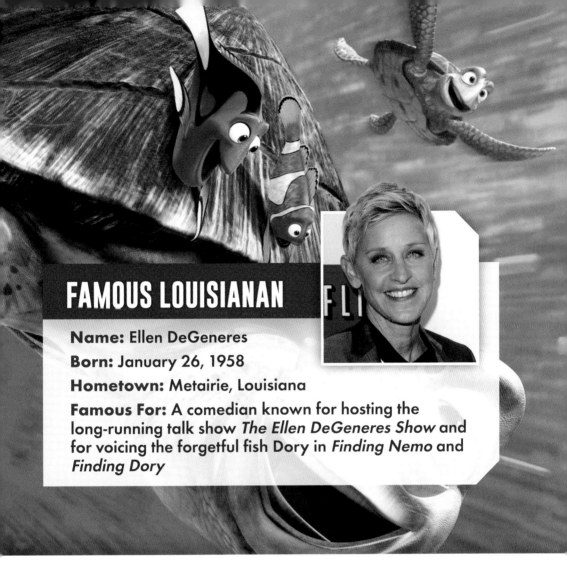

FAMOUS LOUISIANAN

Name: Ellen DeGeneres

Born: January 26, 1958

Hometown: Metairie, Louisiana

Famous For: A comedian known for hosting the long-running talk show *The Ellen DeGeneres Show* and for voicing the forgetful fish Dory in *Finding Nemo* and *Finding Dory*

Creole Louisianans have French, Spanish, Native American, and African American or Black **heritage**. Cajuns come from French Acadians. Most Creoles and Cajuns live in southern Louisiana. Many northern Louisianans claim early English settlers as their **ancestors**. About one in three Louisianans are African American or Black. Smaller numbers of Hispanic Americans, Asian Americans, and Native Americans live in the state. Recent **immigrants** come from Mexico, Honduras, and Vietnam.

   The French built New Orleans along the Mississippi River
in 1718. The city quickly became a major port thanks to its
location near the Gulf of Mexico. Today, downtown
skyscrapers and the French Quarter form the city center.
Historic neighborhood homes mix Spanish and French styles.
Many have balconies overlooking gardens or busy streets.

New Orleans is a center of **culture**. Crowds dance at Preservation Hall and other jazz clubs. Visitors tour the sculpture garden at the New Orleans Museum of Art. A footpath winds through more than 90 works of art. Animal exhibits offer a wild time at the Audubon Zoo.

ALL THAT JAZZ

New Orleans is the birthplace of jazz music. In the early 1900s, African American musicians combined musical styles to create this soulful new sound. Jazz musicians often make up parts of the music as they play.

NEW ORLEANS
MUSEUM OF ART

OIL DRILLING RIG

Farming was Louisiana's first major industry. Today, farmland covers about a quarter of the state. Top crops include sugarcane, rice, and soybeans. Louisiana's waters are an important **resource**. Fishing crews haul in shrimp, crawfish, and oysters.

A BUSY PORT

The Port of South Louisiana stretches along the Mississippi River. It moves more cargo than any other U.S. port.

Offshore, miners drill for oil and natural gas in the Gulf of Mexico. Factory workers make many chemical products. They include plastic, fertilizer, and paint. Most Louisianans hold **service jobs**. They work in schools, banks, and hospitals. In New Orleans, **tourism** employs many service workers in hotels and restaurants.

INVENTED IN LOUISIANA

DENTAL FLOSS
Date Invented: 1815
Inventor: Levi Spear Parmly

BINOCULAR MICROSCOPE
Date Invented: 1852
Inventor: John Riddell

TABASCO SAUCE
Date Invented: 1868
Inventor: Edmund McIlhenny

ZYDECO MUSIC
Date Invented: 1929
Inventor: Amédé Ardoin

JAMBALAYA

Louisiana's food is world famous. Many favorite dishes have Creole and Cajun roots. Spicy jambalaya mixes chicken, sausage, rice, and vegetables. Gumbo is a thick soup that features seafood, sausage, and okra.

GUMBO

Cooks make po'boys with seasoned, fried seafood on French bread. Roast beef is another popular filling. Muffuletta sandwiches layer Italian meats, cheese, and olive salad on round Italian bread. Beignets are often on the menu in New Orleans. Powdered sugar covers these square, deep-fried pastries. Bakers stir up colorful, cinnamon-flavored king cakes during Mardi Gras.

EAT UP!

Many Louisianans are adventurous eaters. They enjoy unique dishes such as frog legs, fried alligator, and rabbit with red beans!

MUFFULETTA SANDWICH

6-8 SERVINGS

Have an adult help you make this tasty sandwich!

INGREDIENTS

1 16-ounce jar of mixed pickled vegetables
1/4 cup chopped pitted green olives, drained
1 clove minced garlic
1 tablespoon olive oil
6 ounces thinly sliced cooked ham
4 ounces thinly sliced salami
4 ounces sliced provolone cheese
1 9-inch round loaf of unsliced Italian bread
black pepper

DIRECTIONS

1. Drain the vegetables, setting aside 2 tablespoons of the liquid. Chop the vegetables.

2. Combine the chopped vegetables, liquid, olives, garlic, and olive oil.

3. Slice the loaf of bread in half horizontally.

4. On the bottom half, layer ham, cheese, and salami. Top with the vegetable mixture.

5. Add the top layer of bread. To serve, cut the sandwich into wedges.

KAYAKING

Louisianans enjoy the great outdoors. They swim and kayak in rivers and lakes. Coastal waters offer deep-sea fishing. Hikers and campers head to Lake Claiborne State Park. The state's wildlife areas draw bird-watchers and photographers.

FISHING

Louisiana history fans tour the Capitol Park Museum in Baton Rouge. The Strand Theater brings musicals to the stage in Shreveport. Many Louisianans listen to jazz and blues at clubs like New Orleans's popular Spotted Cat.

SPOTTED CAT

Football fans cheer for the New Orleans Saints and the Louisiana State University Tigers. Crowds also turn out to watch New Orleans Pelicans basketball games.

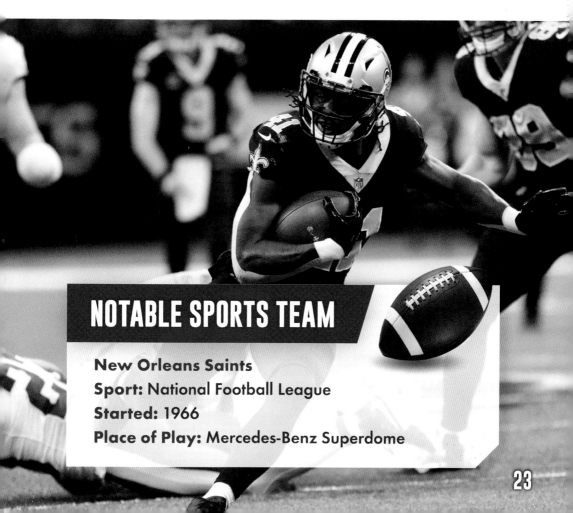

NOTABLE SPORTS TEAM

New Orleans Saints
Sport: National Football League
Started: 1966
Place of Play: Mercedes-Benz Superdome

Louisiana's biggest party is Mardi Gras. People from all over the world travel to New Orleans in the weeks before **Lent** for music, costume balls, and parades. Huge crowds reach for beads and coins tossed from colorful floats. Everyone is welcome to the celebration!

In spring, the New Orleans Jazz and Heritage Fest honors Louisiana's musical roots. Jazz, gospel, blues, and Cajun music fill the air. The Ponchatoula Strawberry Festival in April features berry-eating contests and sack races. In May, crowds at the Breaux Bridge Crawfish Festival eat crawfish boiled, fried, or in stews. Louisianans have a lot to celebrate!

BREAUX BRIDGE CRAWFISH FESTIVAL

MARDI GRAS PARADE
NEW ORLEANS

GOOD LUCK!

Sharing a king cake is a Mardi Gras tradition. Everyone looks for a small toy baby that is baked into the cake. It is said to bring good luck to the person who finds it.

25

LOUISIANA TIMELINE

1861
Louisiana leaves the United States to join the Confederacy during the Civil War but rejoins in 1868

1541
Spanish explorer Hernando de Soto searches the area that is now Louisiana for gold

1812
Louisiana becomes the 18th state

1682
France claims Louisiana

1803
The United States buys Louisiana from France as a part of the Louisiana Purchase

1872

P.B.S. Pinchback serves as acting governor of Louisiana for five weeks, making him the first African American governor in the country

1960

Louisiana schools begin to desegregate

2010

The New Orleans Saints win the Super Bowl

2005

Hurricane Katrina strikes, leaving hundreds of thousands of people homeless

2010

The Deepwater Horizon oil spill in the Gulf of Mexico damages Louisiana's fishing industry

Population

4,657,757 (2020)

Nicknames: The Pelican State, The Bayou State

Motto: Union, Justice, and Confidence

Date of Statehood: April 30, 1812 (the 18th state)

Capital City: Baton Rouge ★

Other Major Cities: New Orleans, Shreveport, Lafayette, Metairie, Lake Charles

Area: 52,378 square miles (135,659 square kilometers); Louisiana is the 31st largest state.

STATE FLAG

Adopted in 1912, the Louisiana state flag features a mother pelican and her young on a blue background. The pelican stands for sacrifice and protection. A banner beneath the pelican shows the state's motto.

INDUSTRY

Main Exports

oil

natural gas

corn

chemicals

rice

soybeans

JOBS

MANUFACTURING
5%

FARMING AND NATURAL RESOURCES
5%

GOVERNMENT
13%

SERVICES
77%

Natural Resources
oil, natural gas, forests, soil, clay, salt, sulfur

GOVERNMENT

8 ELECTORAL VOTES

Federal Government
6 REPRESENTATIVES | **2** SENATORS

USA

LA

State Government
105 REPRESENTATIVES | **39** SENATORS

STATE SYMBOLS

STATE BIRD
BROWN PELICAN

STATE MAMMAL
LOUISIANA BLACK BEAR

STATE FLOWER
MAGNOLIA

STATE TREE
BALD CYPRESS

GLOSSARY

ancestors—relatives who lived long ago

basin—the area drained by a river

bayous—slow-moving streams of water in marshy areas

cathedral—a large Christian church that is the home church of a bishop

culture—the beliefs, arts, and ways of life in a place or society

delta—a land area that forms where a river flows into a large body of water

enslaved—to be considered property and forced to work for no pay

gulf—part of an ocean or sea that extends into land

heritage—the traditions, achievements, and beliefs that are part of the history of a group of people

hurricanes—storms formed in the tropics that have violent winds and often have rain and lightning

immigrants—people who move to a new country

Lent—the time of year when Christians prepare for Easter; Lent begins in February or March and lasts for six weeks.

Louisiana Purchase—a deal made between France and the United States; it gave the United States 828,000 square miles (2,144,510 square kilometers) of land west of the Mississippi River.

plains—large areas of flat land

plantations—large farms that grow cotton, tobacco, sugarcane, and other crops; plantations are mainly found in warm climates.

prairies—large, open areas of grassland

resource—a natural source of income

rural—related to the countryside

service jobs—jobs that perform tasks for people or businesses

settlement—a place where newly arrived people live

tourism—the business of people traveling to visit other places

AT THE LIBRARY

Mack, Larry. *The New Orleans Saints Story.* Minneapolis, Minn.: Bellwether Media, 2017.

O'Brien, Cynthia. *Bringing Back the American Alligator.* New York, N.Y.: Crabtree Publishing, 2019.

Zeiger, Jennifer. *Louisiana.* New York, N.Y.: Children's Press, 2018.

ON THE WEB

FACTSURFER

Factsurfer.com gives you a safe, fun way to find more information.

1. Go to www.factsurfer.com.

2. Enter "Louisiana" into the search box and click 🔍.

3. Select your book cover to see a list of related content.